The House of Mapuhi
Jack London

Published: 1911
Categorie(s): Fiction, Action & Adventure, Short Stories

About London:

Jack London (January 12, 1876 – November 22, 1916), was an American author who wrote The Call of the Wild and other books. A pioneer in the then-burgeoning world of commercial magazine fiction, he was one of the first Americans to make a huge financial success from writing. Source: Wikipedia

Despite the heavy clumsiness of her lines, the Aorai handled easily in the light breeze, and her captain ran her well in be-fore he hove to just outside the suck of the surf. The atoll of Hikueru lay low on the water, a circle of pounded coral sand a hundred yards wide, twenty miles in circumference, and from three to five feet above high-water mark. On the bottom of the huge and glassy lagoon was much pearl shell, and from the deck of the schooner, across the slender ring of the atoll, the divers could be seen at work. But the lagoon had no entrance for even a trading schooner. With a favoring breeze cutters could win in through the tortuous and shallow channel, but the schooners lay off and on outside and sent in their small boats.

The Aorai swung out a boat smartly, into which sprang half a dozen brown-skinned sailors clad only in scarlet loincloths. They took the oars, while in the stern sheets, at the steering sweep, stood a young man garbed in the tropic white that marks the European. The golden strain of Polynesia betrayed itself in the sun-gilt of his fair skin and cast up golden sheens and lights through the glimmering blue of his eyes. Raoul he was, Alexandre Raoul, youngest son of Marie Raoul, the wealthy quarter-caste, who owned and managed half a dozen trading schooners similar to the Aorai. Across an eddy just out-side the entrance, and in and through and over a boiling tide-rip, the boat fought its way to the mirrored calm of the lagoon. Young Raoul leaped out upon the white sand and shook hands with a tall native. The man's chest and shoulders were magnifi-cent, but the stump of a right arm, beyond the flesh of which the age-whitened bone projected several inches, attested the encounter with a shark that had put an end to his diving days and made him a fawner and an intriguer for small favors.

"Have you heard, Alec?" were his first words. "Mapuhi has found a pearl—such a pearl. Never was there one like it ever fished up in Hikueru, nor in all the Paumotus, nor in all the world. Buy it from him. He has it now. And remember that I told you first. He is a fool and you can get it cheap. Have you any tobacco?" Straight up the beach to a shack under a pandanus tree Raoul headed. He was his mother's supercargo, and his

5

business was to comb all the Paumotus for the wealth of copra, shell, and pearls that they yielded up.

He was a young supercargo, it was his second voyage in such capacity, and he suffered much secret worry from his lack of experience in pricing pearls. But when Mapuhi exposed the pearl to his sight he managed to suppress the startle it gave him, and to maintain a careless, commercial expression on his face. For the pearl had struck him a blow. It was large as a pi-geon egg, a perfect sphere, of a whiteness that reflected opalescent lights from all colors about it. It was alive. Never had he seen anything like it. When Mapuhi dropped it into his hand he was surprised by the weight of it. That showed that it was a good pearl. He examined it closely, through a pocket magnifying glass. It was without flaw or blemish. The purity of it seemed almost to melt into the atmosphere out of his hand. In the shade it was softly luminous, gleaming like a tender moon. So translucently white was it, that when he dropped it into a glass of water he had difficulty in finding it. So straight and swiftly had it sunk to the bottom that he knew its weight was excellent.

"Well, what do you want for it?" he asked, with a fine as-sumption of nonchalance.

"I want—" Mapuhi began, and behind him, framing his own dark face, the dark faces of two women and a girl nodded con-currence in what he wanted. Their heads were bent forward, they were animated by a suppressed eagerness, their eyes flashed avariciously.

"I want a house," Mapuhi went on. "It must have a roof of galvanized iron and an octagon-drop-clock. It must be six fathoms long with a porch all around. A big room must be in the centre, with a round table in the middle of it and the octagon-drop-clock on the wall. There must be four bedrooms, two on each side of the big room, and in each bedroom must be an iron bed, two chairs, and a washstand. And back of the house must be a kitchen, a good kitchen, with pots and pans and a stove. And you must build the house on my island, which is Fakarava."

"Is that all?" Raoul asked incredulously.

"There must be a sewing machine," spoke up Tefara, Mapuhi's wife.

"Not forgetting the octagon-drop-clock," added Nauri, Mapuhi's mother.

"Yes, that is all," said Mapuhi.

Young Raoul laughed. He laughed long and heartily. But while he laughed he secretly performed problems in mental arithmetic. He had never built a house in his life, and his no-tions concerning house building were hazy. While he laughed, he calculated the cost of the voyage to Tahiti for materials, of the materials themselves, of the voyage back again to Fakarava, and the cost of landing the materials and of building the house. It would come to four thousand French dollars, al-lowing a margin for safety—four thousand French dollars were equivalent to twenty thousad francs. It was impossible. How was he to know the value of such a pearl? Twenty thousand francs was a lot of money—and of his mother's money at that.

"Mapuhi," he said, "you are a big fool. Set a money price." But Mapuhi shook his head, and the three heads behind him shook with his.

"I want the house," he said. "It must be six fathoms long with a porch all around—"

"Yes, yes," Raoul interrupted. "I know all about your house, but it won't do. I'll give you a thousand Chili dollars."

The four heads chorused a silent negative. "And a hundred Chili dollars in trade."

"I want the house," Mapuhi began.

"What good will the house do you?" Raoul demanded. "The first hurricane that comes along will wash it away. You ought to know.

Captain Raffy says it looks like a hurricane right now."

"Not on Fakarava," said Mapuhi. "The land is much higher there. On this island, yes. Any hurricane can sweep Hikueru. I will have the house on Fakarava. It must be six fathoms long with a porch all around—"

And Raoul listened again to the tale of the house. Several hours he spent in the endeavor to hammer the house obsession out of Mapuhi's mind; but Mapuhi's mother and wife, and Ngakura, Mapuhi's daughter, bolstered him in his resolve for the house. Through the open doorway, while he listened for the twentieth time to the detailed description of the house that was wanted, Raoul saw his schooner's second boat draw up on the beach. The sailors rested on the oars, advertising haste to be gone. The first mate of the Aorai sprang ashore, exchanged a word with the one-armed native, then hurried toward Raoul. The day grew suddenly dark, as a squall obscured the face of the sun. Across the lagoon Raoul could see approaching the ominous line of the puff of wind.

"Captain Raffy says you've got to get to hell outa here," was the mate's greeting. "If there's any shell, we've got to run the risk of picking it up later on—so he says. The barometer's dropped to twenty-nine-seventy."

The gust of wind struck the pandanus tree overhead and tore through the palms beyond, flinging half a dozen ripe cocoanuts with heavy thuds to the ground. Then came the rain out of the distance, advancing with the roar of a gale of wind and causing the water of the lagoon to smoke in driven windrows. The sharp rattle of the first drops was on the leaves when Raoul sprang to his feet.

"A thousand Chili dollars, cash down, Mapuhi," he said. "And two hundred Chili dollars in trade."

"I want a house—" the other began.

"Mapuhi!" Raoul yelled, in order to make himself heard. "You are a fool!"

He flung out of the house, and, side by side with the mate, fought his way down the beach toward the boat. They could not see the boat. The tropic rain sheeted about them so that they could see only the beach under their feet and the spiteful little waves from the lagoon that snapped and bit at the sand. A figure appeared through the deluge. It was Huru-Huru, the man with the one arm.

"Did you get the pearl?" he yelled in Raoul's ear.

"Mapuhi is a fool!" was the answering yell, and the next mo-ment they were lost to each other in the descending water.

Half an hour later, Huru-Huru, watching from the seaward side of the atoll, saw the two boats hoisted in and the Aorai pointing her nose out to sea. And near her, just come in from the sea on the wings of the squall, he saw another schooner hove to and dropping a boat into the water. He knew her. It was the OROHENA, owned by Toriki, the half-caste trader, who served as his own supercargo and who doubtlessly was even then in the stern sheets of the boat. Huru-Huru chuckled.

He knew that Mapuhi owed Toriki for trade goods advanced the year before.

The squall had passed. The hot sun was blazing down, and the lagoon was once more a mirror. But the air was sticky like mucilage, and the weight of it seemed to burden the lungs and make breathing difficult.

"Have you heard the news, Toriki?" Huru-Huru asked. "Mapuhi has found a pearl. Never was there a pearl like it ever fished up in Hikueru, nor anywhere in the Paumotus, nor any-where in all the world. Mapuhi is a fool. Besides, he owes you money. Remember that I told you first. Have you any tobacco?"

And to the grass shack of Mapuhi went Toriki. He was a mas-terful man, withal a fairly stupid one. Carelessly he glanced at the wonderful pearl—glanced for a moment only; and care-lessly he dropped it into his pocket.

"You are lucky," he said. "It is a nice pearl. I will give you credit on the books."

"I want a house," Mapuhi began, in consternation. "It must be six fathoms—"

"Six fathoms your grandmother!" was the trader's retort. "You want to pay up your debts, that's what you want. You owed me twelve hundred dollars Chili. Very well; you owe them no longer. The amount is squared. Besides, I will give you credit for two hundred Chili. If, when I get to Tahiti, the pearl sells well, I will give you credit for another hundred—that will make three hundred. But mind, only if the pearl sells well. I may even lose money on it."

Mapuhi folded his arms in sorrow and sat with bowed head. He had been robbed of his pearl. In place of the house, he had paid a debt. There was nothing to show for the pearl.

"You are a fool," said Tefara.

"You are a fool," said Nauri, his mother. "Why did you let the pearl into his hand?"

"What was I to do?" Mapuhi protested. "I owed him the money. He knew I had the pearl. You heard him yourself ask to see it. I had not told him. He knew. Somebody else told him. And I owed him the money."

"Mapuhi is a fool," mimicked Ngakura. She was twelve years old and did not know any better. Mapuhi relieved his feelings by sending her reeling from a box on the ear; while Tefara and Nauri burst into tears and contin-ued to upbraid him after the manner of women.

Huru-Huru, watching on the beach, saw a third schooner that he knew heave to outside the entrance and drop a boat. It was the Hira, well named, for she was owned by Levy, the Ger-man Jew, the greatest pearl buyer of them all, and, as was well known, Hira was the Tahitian god of fishermen and thieves.

"Have you heard the news?" Huru-Huru asked, as Levy, a fat man with massive asymmetrical features, stepped out upon the beach. "Mapuhi has found a pearl. There was never a pearl like it in Hikueru, in all the Paumotus, in all the world. Mapuhi is a fool. He has sold it to Toriki for fourteen hundred Chili— I listened outside and heard. Toriki is likewise a fool. You can buy it from him cheap. Remember that I told you first. Have you any tobacco?"

"Where is Toriki?"

"In the house of Captain Lynch, drinking absinthe. He has been there an hour."

And while Levy and Toriki drank absinthe and chaffered over the pearl, Huru-Huru listened and heard the stupendous price of twenty-five thousand francs agreed upon.

It was at this time that both the OROHENA and the Hira, running in close to the shore, began firing guns and signalling frantically. The three men stepped outside in time to see the two schooners go hastily about and head off shore, dropping mainsails and flying jibs on the run in the teeth of the squall that heeled them far over on the whitened water. Then the rain blotted them out.

"They'll be back after it's over," said Toriki. "We'd better be getting out of here."

"I reckon the glass has fallen some more," said Captain Lynch.

He was a white-bearded sea-captain, too old for service, who had learned that the only way to live on comfortable terms with his asthma was on Hikueru. He went inside to look at the barometer.

"Great God!" they heard him exclaim, and rushed in to join him at staring at a dial, which marked twenty-nine-twenty. Again they came out, this time anxiously to consult sea and sky. The squall had cleared away, but the sky remained overcast. The two schooners, under all sail and joined by a third, could be seen making back. A veer in the wind induced them to slack off sheets, and five minutes afterward a sudden veer from the opposite quarter caught all three schooners aback, and those on shore could see the boom-tackles being slacked away or cast off on the jump. The sound of the surf was loud, hollow, and menacing, and a heavy swell was setting in. A terrible sheet of lightning burst before their eyes, illuminating the dark day, and the thunder rolled wildly about them.

Toriki and Levy broke into a run for their boats, the latter ambling along like a panic-stricken hippopotamus. As their two boats swept out the entrance, they passed the boat of the Aorai coming in. In the stern sheets, encouraging the rowers, was Raoul. Unable to shake the vision of the pearl from his mind, he was returning to accept Mapuhi's price of a house.

He landed on the beach in the midst of a driving thunder squall that was so dense that he collided with Huru-Huru be-fore he saw him.

"Too late," yelled Huru-Huru. "Mapuhi sold it to Toriki for fourteen hundred Chili, and Toriki sold it to Levy for twenty-five thousand francs. And Levy will sell it in France for a hun-dred thousand francs. Have you any tobacco?"

Raoul felt relieved. His troubles about the pearl were over. He need not worry any more, even if he had not got the pearl. But he did not believe Huru-Huru. Mapuhi might well have sold it for fourteen hundred Chili, but that Levy, who knew pearls, should have paid twenty-five thousand francs was too wide a stretch. Raoul decided to interview Captain Lynch on the sub-ject, but when he arrived at that ancient mariner's house, he found him looking wide-eyed at the barometer.

"What do you read it?" Captain Lynch asked anxiously, rub-bing his spectables and staring again at the instrument.

"Twenty-nine-ten," said Raoul. "I have never seen it so low before."

"I should say not!" snorted the captain. "Fifty years boy and man on all the seas, and I've never seen it go down to that. Listen!"

They stood for a moment, while the surf rumbled and shook the house. Then they went outside. The squall had passed. They could see the Aorai lying becalmed a mile away and pitching and tossing madly in the tremendous seas that rolled in stately procession down out of the northeast and flung themselves furiously upon the coral shore. One of the sailors from the boat pointed at the mouth of the passage and shook his head. Raoul looked and saw a white anarchy of foam and surge.

"I guess I'll stay with you tonight, Captain," he said; then turned to the sailor and told him to haul the boat out and to find shelter for himself and fellows.

"Twenty-nine flat," Captain Lynch reported, coming out from another look at the barometer, a chair in his hand.

He sat down and stared at the spectacle of the sea. The sun came

18

out, increasing the sultriness of the day, while the dead calm still held. The seas continued to increase in magnitude.

"What makes that sea is what gets me," Raoul muttered petulantly.

"There is no wind, yet look at it, look at that fellow there!" Miles in length, carrying tens of thousands of tons in weight, its impact shook the frail atoll like an earthquake. Captain Lynch was startled.

"Gracious!" he bellowed, half rising from his chair, then sink-ing back.

"But there is no wind," Raoul persisted. "I could understand it if there was wind along with it."

"You'll get the wind soon enough without worryin' for it," was the grim reply.

The two men sat on in silence. The sweat stood out on their skin in myriads of tiny drops that ran together, forming blotches of moisture, which, in turn, coalesced into rivulets that dripped to the ground. They panted for breath, the old man's efforts being especially painful. A sea swept up the beach, licking around the trunks of the cocoanuts and subsid-ing almost at their feet.

"Way past high water mark," Captain Lynch remarked; "and I've been here eleven years." He looked at his watch. "It is three o'clock."

A man and woman, at their heels a motley following of brats and curs, trailed disconsolately by. They came to a halt beyond the house, and, after much irresolution, sat down in the sand. A few minutes later another family trailed in from the opposite

direction, the men and women carrying a heterogeneous as-sortment of possessions. And soon several hundred persons of all ages and sexes were congregated about the captain's dwell-ing. He called to one new arrival, a woman with a nursing babe in her arms, and in answer received the information that her house had just been swept into the lagoon.

This was the highest spot of land in miles, and already, in many places on either hand, the great seas were making a clean breach of the slender ring of the atoll and surging into the lagoon. Twenty miles around stretched the ring of the atoll, and in no place was it more than fifty fathoms wide. It was the height of the diving season, and from all the islands around, even as far as Tahiti, the natives had gathered.

"There are twelve hundred men, women, and children here," said Captain Lynch. "I wonder how many will be here tomor-row morning."

"But why don't it blow?—that's what I want to know," Raoul demanded.

"Don't worry, young man, don't worry; you'll get your troubles fast enough."

Even as Captain Lynch spoke, a great watery mass smote the atoll.

The sea water churned about them three inches deep under the chairs. A low wail of fear went up from the many women. The children, with clasped hands, stared at the immense rollers and cried piteously. Chickens and cats, wading per-turbedly in the water, as by common consent, with flight and scramble took refuge on the roof of the captain's house. A Paumotan, with a litter of new-born puppies in a basket, climbed into a cocoanut tree and twenty feet above the ground made the basket fast. The mother floundered about in the wa-ter beneath, whining and yelping.

And still the sun shone brightly and the dead calm continued. They sat and watched the seas and the insane pitching of the Aorai. Captain Lynch gazed at the huge mountains of water sweeping in until he could gaze no more. He covered his face with his hands to shut out the sight; then went into the house.

"Twenty-eight-sixty," he said quietly when he returned.

In his arm was a coil of small rope. He cut it into two-fathom lengths, giving one to Raoul and, retaining one for himself,distributed the remainder among the women with the advice to pick out a tree and climb.

A light air began to blow out of the northeast, and the fan of it on his cheek seemed to cheer Raoul up. He could see the Ao-rai trimming her sheets and heading off shore, and he regret-ted that he was not on her. She would get away at any rate, but as for the atoll—A sea breached across, almost sweeping him off his feet, and he selected a tree. Then he remembered the barometer and ran back to the house. He encountered Captain Lynch on the same errand and together they went in.

"Twenty-eight-twenty," said the old mariner. "It's going to be fair hell around here—what was that?"

The air seemed filled with the rush of something. The house quivered and vibrated, and they heard the thrumming of a mighty note of sound. The windows rattled. Two panes crashed; a draught of wind tore in, striking them and making them stagger. The door opposite banged shut, shattering the latch. The white door knob crumbled in fragments to the floor. The room's walls bulged like a gas balloon in the process of sudden inflation. Then came a new sound like the rattle of mus-ketry, as the spray from a sea struck the wall of the house. Captain Lyncyh looked at his watch. It was four o'clock. He put on a coat of pilot cloth, unhooked the barometer, and stowed it away in a capacious pocket. Again a sea struck the house, with a heavy thud, and the light building tilted, twisted, quarter around on its foundation, and sank down, its floor at an angle of ten degrees.

Raoul went out first. The wind caught him and whirled him away. He noted that it had hauled around to the east. With a great effort he threw himself on the sand, crouching and hold-ing his own. Captain Lynch, driven like a wisp of straw, sprawled over him. Two of the Aorai'S sailors, leaving a cocoa-nut tree to which they had been clinging, came to their aid, leaning against the wind at impossible angles and fighting and clawing every inch of the way.

The old man's joints were stiff and he could not climb, so the sailors, by means of short ends of rope tied together, hoisted him up the trunk, a few feet at a time, till they could make him fast, at the top of the tree, fifty feet from the ground. Raoul passed his length of rope around the base of an adjacent tree and stood looking on. The wind was frightful. He had never dreamed it could blow so hard. A sea breached across the atoll, wetting him to the knees ere it subsided into the lagoon. The sun had disappeared, and a lead-colored twilight settled down. A few drops of rain, driving horizontally, struck him. The im-pact was like that of leaden pellets. A splash of salt spray struck his face. It was like the slap of a man's hand. His cheeks stung, and involuntary tears of pain were in his smarting eyes. Several hundred natives had taken to the trees, and he could have laughed at the bunches of human fruit clustering in the tops. Then, being

Tahitian-born, he doubled his body at the waist, clasped the trunk of his tree with his hands, pressed the soles of his feet against the near surface of the trunk, and began to walk up the tree. At the top he found two women, two children, and a man. One little girl clasped a housecat in her arms.

From his eyrie he waved his hand to Captain Lynch, and that doughty patriarch waved back. Raoul was appalled at the sky. It had approached much nearer—in fact, it seemed just over his head; and it had turned from lead to black. Many people were still on the ground grouped about the bases of the trees and holding on. Several such clusters were praying, and in one the Mormon missionary was exhorting. A weird sound, rhythmical, faint as the faintest chirp of a far cricket, enduring but for a moment, but in the moment suggesting to him vaguely the thought of heaven and celestial music, came to his ear. He glanced about him and saw, at the base of another tree, a large cluster of

26

people holding on by ropes and by one another. He could see their faces working and their lips moving in unison. No sound came to him, but he knew that they were singing hymns.

Still the wind continued to blow harder. By no conscious pro-cess could he measure it, for it had long since passed beyond all his experience of wind; but he knew somehow, nevertheless, that it was blowing harder. Not far away a tree was uprooted, flinging its load of human beings to the ground. A sea washed across the strip of sand, and they were gone. Things were hap-pening quickly. He saw a brown shoulder and a black head sil-houetted against the churning white of the lagoon. The next in-stant that, too, had vanished. Other trees were going, falling and criss-crossing like matches. He was amazed at the power of the wind. His own tree was swaying perilously, one woman was wailing and clutching the little girl, who in turn still hung on to the cat.

The man, holding the other child, touched Raoul's arm and pointed.

He looked and saw the Mormon church careering drunkenly a hundred feet away. It had been torn from its foundations, and wind and sea were heaving and shoving it to-ward the lagoon. A frightful wall of water caught it, tilted it, and flung it against half a dozen cocoanut trees. The bunches of human fruit fell like ripe cocoanuts. The subsiding wave showed them on the ground, some lying motionless, others squirming and writhing. They reminded him strangely of ants. He was not shocked. He had risen above horror. Quite as a matter of course he noted the succeeding wave sweep the sand clean of the human wreckage. A third wave, more colossal than any he had yet seen, hurled the church into the lagoon, where it floated off into the obscurity to leeward, half-submerged, re-minding him for all the world of a Noah's ark.

He looked for Captain Lynch's house, and was surprised to find it gone. Things certainly were happening quickly. He no-ticed that many of the people in the trees that still held had descended to the ground. The wind had yet again increased. His own tree showed that. It no longer swayed or bent over and back. Instead, it remained practically stationary, curved in a rigid angle from the wind and merely vibrating. But the vi-bration was sickening. It was like that of a tuning-fork or the tongue of a jew's-harp. It was the rapidity of the vibration that made it so bad. Even though its roots held, it could not stand the strain for long. Something would have to break.

Ah, there was one that had gone. He had not seen it go, but there it stood, the remnant, broken off half-way up the trunk. One did not know what happened unless he saw it. The mere crashing of trees and wails of human despair occupied no place in that mighty volume of sound. He chanced to be looking in Captain Lynch's direction when it happened. He saw the trunk of the tree, half-way up, splinter and part without noise. The head of the tree, with three sailors of the Aorai and the old captain sailed off over the lagoon. It did not fall to the ground, but drove through the air like a piece of chaff. For a hundred yards he followed its flight, when it struck the water. He strained his eyes, and was sure that he saw Captain Lynch wave farewell.

Raoul did not wait for anything more. He touched the native and made signs to descend to the ground. The man was willing, but his women were paralayzed from terror, and he elected to remain with them. Raoul passed his rope around the tree and slid down. A rush of salt water went over his head. He held his breath and clung desperately to the rope. The water subsided, and in the shelter of the trunk he breathed once more. He fastened the rope more securely, and then was put under by another sea. One of the women slid down and joined him, the native remaining by the other woman, the two children, and the cat.

The supercargo had noticed how the groups clinging at the bases of the other trees continually diminished. Now he saw the process work out alongside him. It required all his strength to hold on, and the woman who had joined him was growing weaker. Each time he emerged from a sea he was surprised to find himself still there, and next, surprised to find the woman still there. At last he emerged to find himself alone. He looked up. The top of the tree had gone as well. At half its original height, a splintered end vibrated. He was safe. The roots still held, while the tree had been shorn of its windage. He began to climb up. He was so weak that he went slowly, and sea after sea caught him before he was above them. Then he tied him-self to the trunk and stiffened his soul to face the night and he knew not what.

He felt very lonely in the darkness. At times it seemed to him that it was the end of the world and that he was the last one left alive. Still the wind increased. Hour after hour it increased. By what he calculated was eleven o'clock, the wind had be-come unbelievable. It was a horrible, monstrous thing, a screaming fury, a wall that smote and passed on but that con-tinued to smite and pass on—a wall without end. It seemed to him that he had become light and ethereal; that it was he that was in motion; that he was being driven with inconceivable ve-locity through unending solidness. The wind was no longer air in motion. It had become substantial as water or quicksilver. He had a feeling that he could reach into it and tear it out in chunks as one might do with the meat in the carcass of a steer; that he could seize hold of the wind and hang on to it as a man might hang on to the face of a cliff.

The wind strangled him. He could not face it and breathe, for it rushed in through his mouth and nostrils, distending his lungs like bladders. At such moments it seemed to him that his body was being packed and swollen with solid earth. Only by pressing his lips to the trunk of the tree could he breathe. Also, the ceaseless impact of the wind exhausted him. Body and brain became wearied. He no longer observed, no longer thought, and was but semiconscious. One idea constituted his consciousness: SO THIS WAS A HURRICANE. That one idea persisted irregularly. It was like a feeble flame that flickered occasionally. From a state of stupor he would return to it—SO THIS WAS A HURRICANE. Then he would go off into another stupor.

The height of the hurricane endured from eleven at night till three in the morning, and it was at eleven that the tree in which clung Mapuhi and his women snapped off. Mapuhi rose to the surface of the lagoon, still clutching his daughter Ngak-ura. Only a South Sea islander could have lived in such a driv-ing smother. The pandanus tree, to which he attached himself, turned over and over in the froth and churn; and it was only by holding on at times and waiting, and at other times shifting his grips rapidly, that he was able to get his head and Ngakura's to the surface at intervals sufficiently near together to keep the breath in them. But the air was mostly water, what with flying spray and sheeted rain that poured along at right angles to the perpendicular.

It was ten miles across the lagoon to the farther ring of sand. Here, tossing tree trunks, timbers, wrecks of cutters, and wreckage of houses, killed nine out of ten of the miserable be-ings who survived the passage of the lagoon. Half-drowned, ex-hausted, they were hurled into this mad mortar of the elements and battered into formless flesh. But Mapuhi was fortunate. His chance was the one in ten; it fell to him by the freakage of fate. He emerged upon the sand, bleeding from a score of wounds.
Ngakura's left arm was broken; the fingers of her right hand were crushed; and cheek and forehead were laid open to the bone. He clutched a tree that yet stood, and clung on, holding the girl and sobbing for air, while the waters of the lagoon washed by knee-high and at times waist-high.

At three in the morning the backbone of the hurricane broke. By five no more than a stiff breeze was blowing. And by six it was dead calm and the sun was shining. The sea had gone down. On the yet restless edge of the lagoon, Mapuhi saw the broken bodies of those that had failed in the landing. Undoubtedly Tefara and Nauri were among them. He went along the beach examining them, and came upon his wife, lying half in and half out of the water. He sat down and wept, mak-ing harsh animal noises after the manner of primitive grief. Then she stirred uneasily, and groaned. He looked more closely. Not only was she alive, but she was uninjured. She was merely sleeping. Hers also had been the one chance in ten.

Of the twelve hundred alive the night before but three hun-dred remained. The mormon missionary and a gendarme made the census. The lagoon was cluttered with corpses. Not a house nor a hut was standing. In the whole atoll not two stones remained one upon another. One in fifty of the cocoanut palms still stood, and they were wrecks, while on not one of them re-mained a single nut.

There was no fresh water. The shallow wells that caught the surface seepage of the rain were filled with salt. Out of the la-goon a few soaked bags of flour were recovered. The survivors cut the hearts out of the fallen cocoanut trees and ate them. Here and there they crawled into tiny hutches, made by hol-lowing out the sand and covering over with fragments of metal roofing. The missionary made a crude still, but he could not distill water for three hundred persons. By the end of the second day, Raoul, taking a bath in the lagoon, discovered that his thirst was somewhat relieved. He cried out the news, and thereupon three hundred men, women, and children could have been seen, standing up to their necks in the lagoon and trying to drink water in through their skins. Their dead floated about them, or were stepped upon where they still lay upon the bottom. On the third day the people buried their dead and sat down to wait for the rescue steamers.

In the meantime, Nauri, torn from her family by the hur-ricane, had been swept away on an adventure of her own. Clinging to a rough plank that wounded and bruised her and that filled her body with splinters, she was thrown clear over the atoll and carried away to sea. Here, under the amazing buf-fets of mountains of water, she lost her plank. She was an old woman nearly sixty; but she was Paumotan-born, and she had never been out of sight of the sea in her life. Swimming in the darkness, strangling, suffocating, fighting for air, she was struck a heavy blow on the shoulder by a cocoanut. On the in-stant her plan was formed, and she seized the nut. In the next hour she captured seven more. Tied together, they formed a life-buoy that preserved her life while at the same time it threatened to pound her to a jelly. She was a fat woman, and she bruised easily; but she had had experience of hurricanes, and while she prayed to her shark god for protection from sharks, she waited for the wind to break. But at three o'clock she was in such a stupor that she did not know. Nor did she know at six o'clock when the dead calm settled down. She was shocked into consciousness when she was thrown upon the sand. She dug in with raw and bleeding hands and feet and clawed against the backwash until she was beyond the reach of the waves.

She knew where she was. This land could be no other than the tiny islet of Takokota. It had no lagoon. No one lived upon it.

Hikueru was fifteen miles away. She could not see Hikueru, but she knew that it lay to the south. The days went by, and she lived on the cocoanuts that had kept her afloat. They sup-plied her with drinking water and with food. But she did not drink all she wanted, nor eat all she wanted. Rescue was prob-lematical. She saw the smoke of the rescue steamers on the ho-rizon, but what steamer could be expected to come to lonely, uninhabited Takokota?

From the first she was tormented by corpses. The sea per-sisted in flinging them upon her bit of sand, and she persisted, until her strength failed, in thrusting them back into the sea where the sharks tore at them and devoured them. When her strength failed, the bodies festooned her beach with ghastly horror, and she withdrew from them as far as she could, which was not far. By the tenth day her last cocoanut was gone, and she was shrivelling from thirst. She dragged herself along the sand, looking for cocoanuts. It was strange that so many bodies floated up, and no nuts. Surely, there were more cocoanuts afloat than dead men! She gave up at last, and lay exhausted. The end had come. Nothing remained but to wait for death.

Coming out of a stupor, she became slowly aware that she was gazing at a patch of sandy-red hair on the head of a corpse. The sea flung the body toward her, then drew it back. It turned over, and she saw that it had no face. Yet there was something familiar about that patch of sandy-red hair. An hour passed. She did not exert herself to make the identification. She was waiting to die, and it mattered little to her what man that thing of horror once might have been.

But at the end of the hour she sat up slowly and stared at the corpse. An unusually large wave had thrown it beyond the reach of the lesser waves. Yes, she was right; that patch of red hair could belong to but one man in the Paumotus. It was Levy, the German Jew, the man who had bought the pearl and carried it away on the Hira. Well, one thing was evident: The Hira had been lost. The pearl buyer's god of fishermen and thieves had gone back on him.

She crawled down to the dead man. His shirt had been torn away, and she could see the leather money belt about his waist. She held her breath and tugged at the buckles. They gave easier than she had expected, and she crawled hurriedly away across the sand, dragging the belt after her. Pocket after pocket she unbuckled in the belt and found empty. Where could he have put it? In the last pocket of all she found it, the first and only pearl he had bought on the voyage. She crawled a few feet farther, to escape the pestilence of the belt, and ex-amined the pearl. It was the one Mapuhi had found and been robbed of by Toriki. She weighed it in her hand and rolled it back and forth caressingly. But in it she saw no intrinsic beauty. What she did see was the house Mapuhi and Tefara and she had builded so carefully in their minds. Each time she looked at the pearl she saw the house in all its details, includ-ing the octagon-drop-clock on the wall. That was something to live for. She tore a strip from her ahu and tied the pearl securely about her neck. Then she went on along the beach, panting and groaning, but resolutely seeking for cocoanuts. Quickly she found one, and, as she glanced around, a second. She broke one, drinking its water, which was mildewy, and eating the last particle of the meat. A little later she found a shattered dugout. Its outrigger was gone, but she was hopeful, and, be-fore the day was out, she found the outrigger. Every find was an augury. The pearl was a talisman. Late in the afternoon she saw a wooden box floating low in the water. When she dragged it out on the beach its contents rattled, and inside she found ten tins of salmon. She opened one by hammering it on the ca-noe. When a leak was started, she drained the tin. After that she spent several hours in extracting the salmon, hammering and squeezing it out a morsel at a time.

Eight days longer she waited for rescue. In the meantime she fastened the outrigger back on the canoe, using for lashings all the cocoanut fibre she could find, and also what remained of her ahu. The canoe was badly cracked, and she could not make it water-tight; but a calabash made from a cocoanut she stored on board for a bailer. She was hard put for a paddle. With a piece of tin she sawed off all her hair close to the scalp. Out of the hair she braided a cord; and by means of the cord she lashed a three-foot piece of broom handle to a board from the salmon case.

She gnawed wedges with her teeth and with them wedged the lashing.

On the eighteenth day, at midnight, she launched the canoe through the surf and started back for Hikueru. She was an old woman. Hardship had stripped her fat from her till scarcely more than bones and skin and a few stringy muscles remained. The canoe was large and should have been paddled by three strong men.

But she did it alone, with a make-shift paddle. Also, the ca-noe leaked badly, and one-third of her time was devoted to bailing. By clear daylight she looked vainly for Hikueru. Astern, Takokota had sunk beneath the sea rim. The sun blazed down on her nakedness, compelling her body to surrender its mois-ture. Two tins of salmon were left, and in the course of the day she battered holes in them and drained the liquid. She had no time to waste in extracting the meat. A current was setting to the westward, she made westing whether she made southing or not.

In the eary afternoon, standing upright in the canoe, she sighted Hikueru Its wealth of cocoanut palms was gone. Only here and there, at wide intervals, could she see the ragged remnants of trees. The sight cheered her. She was nearer than she had thought. The current was setting her to the westward. She bore up against it and paddled on. The wedges in the paddle lashing worked loose, and she lost much time, at fre-quent intervals, in driving them tight. Then there was the bail-ing. One hour in three she had to cease paddling in order to bail. And all the time she driftd to the westward.

By sunset Hikueru bore southeast from her, three miles away. There was a full moon, and by eight o'clock the land was due east and two miles away. She struggled on for another hour, but the land was as far away as ever. She was in the main grip of the current; the canoe was too large; the paddle was too inadequate; and too much of her time and strength was wasted in bailing. Besides, she was very weak and growing weaker. Despite her efforts, the canoe was drifting off to the westward.

She breathed a prayer to her shark god, slipped over the side, and began to swim. She was actually refreshed by the wa-ter, and quickly left the canoe astern. At the end of an hour the land was perceptibly nearer. Then came her fright. Right be-fore her eyes, not twenty feet away, a large fin cut the water. She swam steadily toward it, and slowly it glided away, curving off toward the right and circling around her. She kept her eyes on the fin and swam on. When the fin disappeared, she lay face downward in the water and watched. When the fin reappeared she resumed her swimming. The monster was lazy— she could see that. Without doubt he had been well fed since the hur-ricane. Had he been very hungry, she knew he would not have hesitated from making a dash for her. He was fifteen feet long, and one bite, she knew, could cut her in half.

But she did not have any time to waste on him. Whether she swam or not, the current drew away from the land just the same. A half hour went by, and the shark began to grow bolder. Seeing no harm in her he drew closer, in narrowing circles, cocking his eyes at her impudently as he slid past. Sooner or later, she knew well enough, he would get up suffi-cient courage to dash at her. She resolved to play first. It was a desperate act she meditated. She was an old woman, alone in the sea and weak from starvation and hardship; and yet she, in the face of this sea tiger, must anticipate his dash by herself dashing at him. She swam on, waiting her chance. At last he passed languidly by, barely eight feet away. She rushed at him suddenly, feigning that she was attacking him. He gave a wild flirt of his tail as he fled away, and his sandpaper hide, striking her, took off her skin from elbow to shoulder. He swam rapidly, in a widening circle, and at last disappeared.

In the hole in the sand, covered over by fragments of metal roofing, Mapuhi and Tefara lay disputing.

"If you had done as I said," charged Tefara, for the thou-sandth time, "and hidden the pearl and told no one, you would have it now."

"But Huru-Huru was with me when I opened the shell—have I not told you so times and times and times without end?"

"And now we shall have no house. Raoul told me today that if you had not sold the pearl to Toriki—"

"I did not sell it. Toriki robbed me."

"—that if you had not sold the pearl, he would give you five thousand French dollars, which is ten thousand Chili."

"He has been talking to his mother," Mapuhi explained. "She has an eye for a pearl."

"And now the pearl is lost," Tefara complained.

"It paid my debt with Toriki. That is twelve hundred I have made, anyway."

"Toriki is dead," she cried. "They have heard no word of his schooner. She was lost along with the Aorai and the Hira. Will Toriki pay you the three hundred credit he promised? No, be-cause Toriki is dead. And had you found no pearl, would you today owe Toriki the twelve hundred? No, because Toriki is dead, and you cannot pay dead men."

"But Levy did not pay Toriki," Mapuhi said. "He gave him a piece of paper that was good for the money in Papeete; and now Levy is dead and cannot pay; and Toriki is dead and the paper lost with him, and the pearl is lost with Levy. You are

right, Tefara. I have lost the pearl, and got nothing for it. Now let us sleep."

He held up his hand suddenly and listened. From without came a noise, as of one who breathed heavily and with pain. A hand fumbled against the mat that served for a door.

"Who is there?" Mapuhi cried.

"Nauri," came the answer. "Can you tell me where is my son, Mapuhi?"

Tefara screamed and gripped her husband's arm. "A ghost! she chattered. "A ghost!"

Mapuhi's face was a ghastly yellow. He clung weakly to his wife.

"Good woman," he said in faltering tones, striving to disguise his vice, "I know your son well. He is living on the east side of the lagoon."

From without came the sound of a sigh. Mapuhi began to feel elated. He had fooled the ghost.

"But where do you come from, old woman?" he asked. "From the sea," was the dejected answer.

"I knew it! I knew it!" screamed Tefara, rocking to and fro. "Since when has Tefara bedded in a strange house?" came Nauri's voice through the matting.

Mapuhi looked fear and reproach at his wife. It was her voice that had betrayed them.

"And since when has Mapuhi, my son, denied his old moth-er?" the voice went on.

"No, no, I have not—Mapuhi has not denied you," he cried. "I am not Mapuhi. He is on the east end of the lagoon, I tell you."

Ngakura sat up in bed and began to cry. The matting started to shake.

"What are you doing?" Mapuhi demanded. "I am coming in," said the voice of Nauri.

One end of the matting lifted. Tefara tried to dive under the blankets, but Mapuhi held on to her. He had to hold on to something. Together, struggling with each other, with shiver-ing bodies and chattering teeth, they gazed with protruding eyes at the lifting mat. They saw Nauri, dripping with sea wa-ter, without her ahu, creep in. They rolled over backward from her and fought for Ngakura's blanket with which to cover their heads.

50

"You might give your old mother a drink of water," the ghost said plaintively.

"Give her a drink of water," Tefara commanded in a shaking voice.

"Give her a drink of water," Mapuhi passed on the command to Ngakura.

And together they kicked out Ngakura from under the blanket. A minute later, peeping, Mapuhi saw the ghost drink-ing. When it reached out a shaking hand and laid it on his, he felt the weight of it and was convinced that it was no ghost. Then he emerged, dragging Tefara after him, and in a few minutes all were listening to Nauri's tale. And when she told of Levy, and dropped the pearl into Tefara's hand, even she was reconciled to the reality of her mother-in-law.

"In the morning," said Tefara, "you will sell the pearl to Raoul for five thousand French."

"The house?" objected Nauri.

"He will build the house," Tefara answered. "He ways it will cost four thousand French. Also will he give one thousand French in credit, which is two thousand Chili."

"And it will be six fathoms long?" Nauri queried. "Ay," answered Mapuhi, "six fathoms."

"And in the middle room will be the octagon-drop-clock?" "Ay, and the round table as well."

"Then give me something to eat, for I am hungry," said Nauri, complacently. "And after that we will sleep, for I am weary. And tomorrow we will have more talk about the house before we sell the pearl. It will be better if we take the thou-sand French in cash. Money is ever better than credit in buying goods from the traders."

CPSIA information can be obtained
at www.ICGtesting.com
Printed in the USA
LVHW020918190221
679456LV00037B/709